Shirley H. Ruinger

Alistair Owl

Alistair Owl Was Napping at Noon

by Craig Risinger

illustrations by Shirley H. Risinger

ISBN: 978-0-9990377-0-6

First edition, printed 2017.

Fonts used include *English Script* and Crimson Text.

Thanks, Mom — for the images and for everything.

The character in this book is entirely fictional. Any resemblance to owls living or dead is purely coincidental.

For some very dear young people:
Abby, Aaron, Brynn, Carly, and Kevin

Alistair Owl

was napping

at noon.

He'd stayed up **all** night

refining a tune

he'd been whistling for weeks
while he hunted for mice.

The rhythm was catchy,
the melody nice,

but the harmony
still didn't *quite* satisfy.

Could he make it
still better?

He knew
he could try!

So he worked

and he struggled

and never

got bored:

He tried chord

after <u>chord</u>

after **chord**

after <u>***chord***</u> —

but he just couldn't find it,
        and now he felt pooped.
His wings and his eyelids
        grew heavy and drooped.

His get-up-and-go
        had got up and gone;
the switch in his brain
        changed to Off (off of On).

So he fumbled
               and trundled

and

stumbled

to bed,

slipped himself

    under covers

        and rested

           his head.

The morning sky
        changed,
                red to pink,
                        then light rose,
        as the sun shone
            on Alistair's silent repose.

But the work

    that he'd done

        had not all been in vain:

It kept cooking

        in Alistair's

            unconscious brain.

His subconscious
finished

what his conscious mind
started.

When he finally awoke,

he arose happy-hearted.

His

fine feathers **fluttered**

as his

full wings **flapped fast!**

He'd dreamed

up the answer.

He'd **found** it

at last!

He *flew* to the piano

and pressed on the keys...

and grinned as he heard

his *ideal*

harmonies.